# Itsy Bitsy Spider

# Itsy Bitsy Spider

by **Keith Chapman**

*Illustrated by* **Jack Tickle**

SCHOLASTIC INC.

New York Toronto London Auckland Sydney
Mexico City New Delhi Hong Kong Buenos Aires

**whooosh!**

Itsy Bitsy Spider,
playing on a farm.
Spinning silver silk webs,
high up in a barn.

From an open window,
a gust of wind blows WHOOOSH!

# Swooooosh!

And Itsy Bitsy Spider
with a SWOOOOOSH
goes, too!

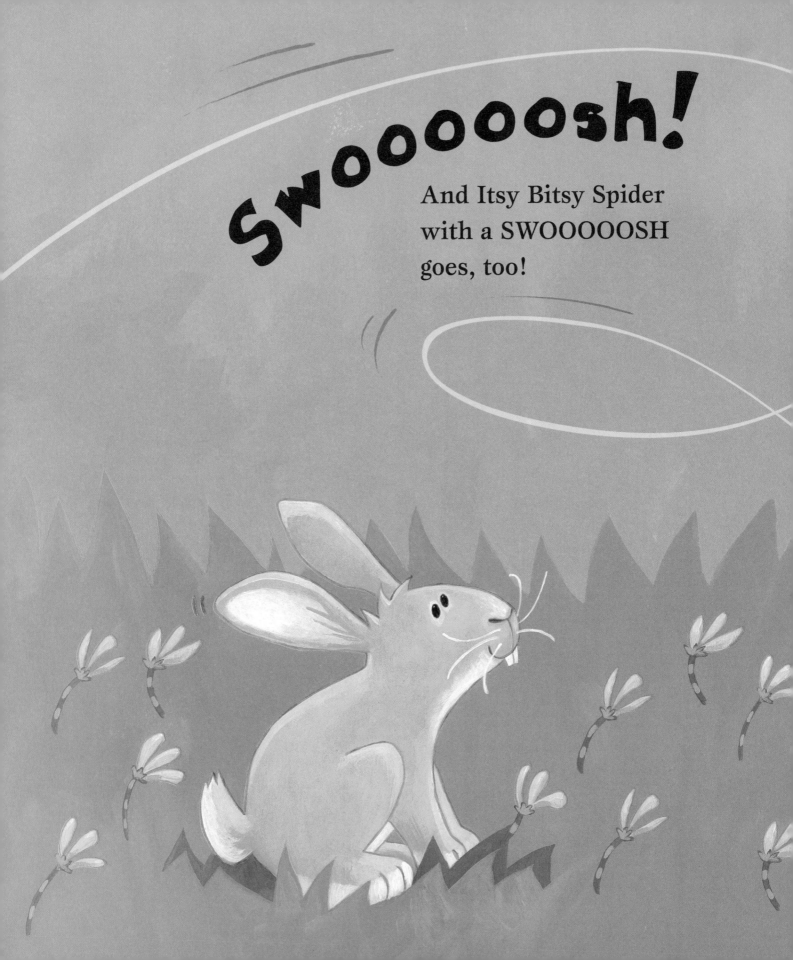

Itsy Bitsy Spider
is flying, there he goes!
He drifts on to a pink pig
and dangles from its nose.

OINKKK! grunts the pig
with Itsy climbing up his snout.
And Itsy Bitsy Spider
is catapulted out!

Oinkkk!

Itsy Bitsy Spider,
he doesn't think it's funny.
He's tangled on a gray goat
and calls out for his mommy.

B-E-H-H-H-H-H! bleats the goat,
who shakes from side to side.
And Itsy Bitsy Spider
begins another ride!

Behhhhh!

Itsy Bitsy Spider,
can you see him now?
He's fluttered on to Buttercup,
the black-and-white young cow.

MOOOO! says Buttercup
and flicks her long, wide ears.
And Itsy Bitsy Spider
spins off and disappears!

MOOOO!

Itsy Bitsy Spider,
gliding through the air.
He hangs on to a duck's bill
and tickles under there.

QUACK! honks the yellow duck,
and gives a great big sneeze.
And Itsy Bitsy Spider
floats off in the breeze!

Quack!

Itsy Bitsy Spider,
what a dizzy day!
He's settled on a brown horse
chewing clumps of hay.

Neig

NEIGHHHH! snorts the horse,
and jumps up really high.
Then Itsy Bitsy Spider
takes off through the sky!

hhhh!

Itsy Bitsy Spider,
clever little thing.
He shoots out lines of web silk
and sticks to rooster's wing.

Cock-a-doodle-doo!

The red, feathered
rooster crows
COCK-A-DOODLE-DOO!
But Itsy Bitsy Spider,
where on earth are you?

Itsy Bitsy Spider,
what's he stuck on now?
A goat, horse, or rooster?
A pig, duck, or cow?

No, he bounces with a

# Boinnggg!

Hooray! It's Mommy's web!
Now Itsy Bitsy Spider
is safely home in bed!

ISBN 0-439-80750-6

Text copyright © 2006 by Keith Chapman. Illustrations copyright © 2006 by Jack Tickle. All
rights reserved. Published by Scholastic Inc., 557 Broadway, New York, NY 10012,
by arrangement with Tiger Tales, an imprint of ME Media LLC. SCHOLASTIC
and associated logos are trademarks and/or registered trademarks of Scholastic Inc.

12 11 10 9 8 7 6 5 4 3 2 1                                    5 6 7 8 9 10/0

Printed in the U.S.A.                                   40

First Scholastic printing, October 2005